THE PUMPKIN BLANKET

Deborah Turney Zagwyn

Tricycle Press
Berkeley, California

The Pumpkin Blanket

TRICYCLE PRESS
P.O. Box 7123
Berkeley, California 94707

Design: Word & Image Design Studio Inc.

The Library of Congress has catalogued an earlier edition as follows:

Zagwÿn, Deborah Turney.
   The pumpkin blanket.
   Summary: A little girl sacrifices her beloved blanket to save the
pumpkins in the garden from frost.
   [1. Blankets—Fiction. 2. Pumpkin—Fiction]
I. Title
PZ7.Z245Pu 1990   [E]   90–15012
ISBN 0-89087-637-1

First published by Celestial Arts, 1990

First Tricycle Press printing, 1997
ISBN 1-883672-63-5 (hardcover)
ISBN 1-883672-59-7 (paperback)
Printed in Singapore

1 2 3 4 5 6 7 — 01 00 99 98 97

For my fair friend Carol, who gave her blanket to the cabbages
when she was just-past-small, on-her-way-to-Big
and
For those with precious blanket memories of their own

When Clee was born, the Northern Lights shook their folds above her bed, but no one saw them.

Clee's family only had eyes for Clee.

Later the door blew open, and the wind tossed a blanket inside. Swish! No one heard.

Clee's family only had ears for Clee.

Her mother called the blanket a gift, but could not remember who had given it.

"An Aunt!" Clee's Mother guessed.

"A shy but friendly neighbor!" ventured an aunt.

Clee's father said nothing. He thought the sunny-colored squares of the blanket looked surprisingly like his garden patch.

"Let's call it the pumpkin blanket," he suggested, because round baby Clee looked a lot like a pumpkin bundled up in it.

The pumpkin blanket was a close friend to little Clee, light and warm around her body, soft and dreamy between her fingers, smooth under her cheek.

One cold winter's night, when the garden had a snowy blanket of its own, Clee, who was three, peered out her bedroom window. She could see the coyotes sniffing and pawing the frozen compost heap. Clee shivered as they raced back, yipping and yowling through the birch tree skeletons into the dark forest behind. Only the treasured pumpkin blanket wrapped about her ears could stifle their voices. It was coyote-proof.

One hot summer's afternoon when the garden was abuzz with insect excitement, Clee, who was four, sorted through the compost pile rottings for baby worms. Later, when one escaped from her shirt pocket at the dinner table, Clee was scolded and sent upstairs. There the pumpkin blanket was waiting and covered her like a tent. Peeking out from underneath, Clee saw folds like distant mountains and wrinkles like waves on a patchwork lake.

One day, late in September, Clee, who was five, was dancing with her blanket by the garden.

Sometimes it was her cape or it was her swirling skirt. Sometimes she held it high in the sky to flutter like the autumn leaves.

Clee's father was busy in the garden rows, harvesting the vegetables. One by one the bright-colored patches disappeared into buckets. Green leaves were piled on the compost heap. Soon all that remained were the pumpkins.

lee's father leaned on his shovel. Clee would go to kindergarten at the local school after Christmas. She could not carry her pumpkin blanket to class. The other children would tease her when she stroked the satin edges, soft and dreamy and smooth under her cheek.

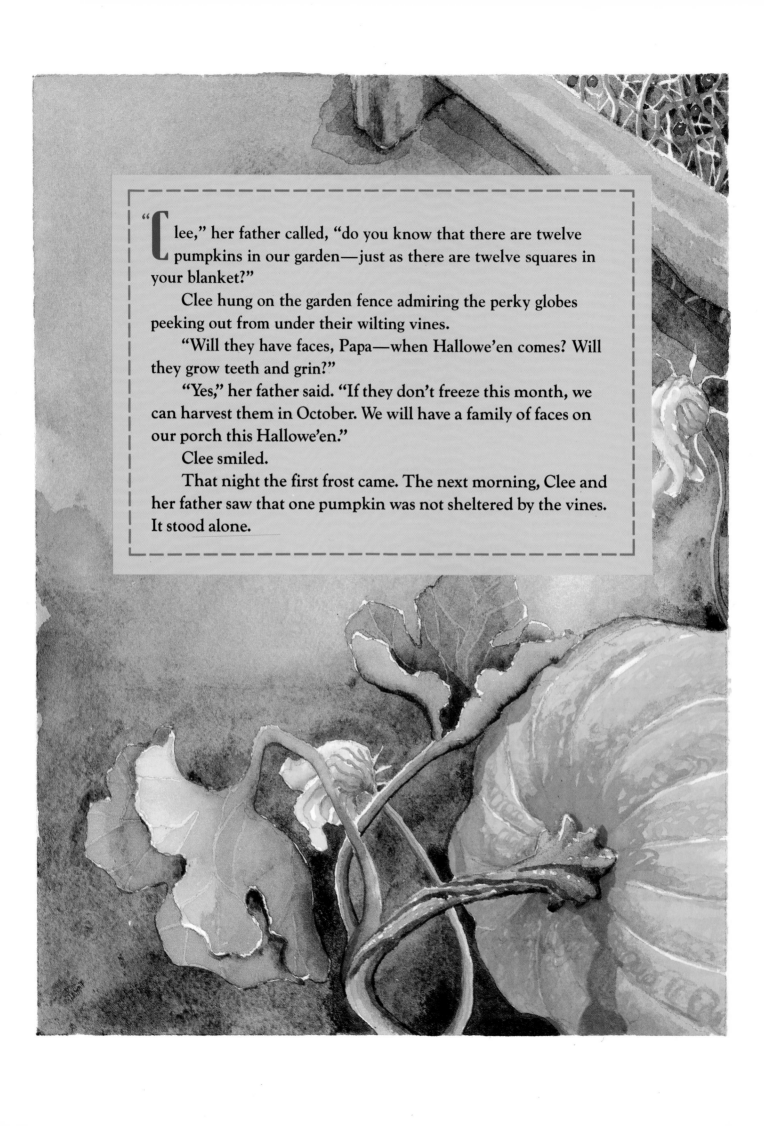

"Clee," her father called, "do you know that there are twelve pumpkins in our garden—just as there are twelve squares in your blanket?"

Clee hung on the garden fence admiring the perky globes peeking out from under their wilting vines.

"Will they have faces, Papa—when Hallowe'en comes? Will they grow teeth and grin?"

"Yes," her father said. "If they don't freeze this month, we can harvest them in October. We will have a family of faces on our porch this Hallowe'en."

Clee smiled.

That night the first frost came. The next morning, Clee and her father saw that one pumpkin was not sheltered by the vines. It stood alone.

"Clee," her father asked, "will you share your blanket with the pumpkins? One square would cover that shivering pumpkin and save it from the frost."

A lump came to Clee's throat but she nodded. Then her father reached for his pocketknife and carefully cut the threads, separating a square from the pumpkin blanket. Gently Clee covered the pumpkin.

The next morning Clee and her father hurried to the pumpkin patch. There was the pumpkin, plump as a melon under its little square shawl. It had survived the frost. But another pumpkin had become exposed as the vines fell away. Clee knew that without a cover the frost would bite it hard. She gave up one more square from her pumpkin blanket.

Night after night the cold nipped at the garden. Night after night Clee gave another square to another pumpkin to keep its head warm. In the early October night sky the Northern Lights began to flicker faintly again.

Finally Clee had only one square left. It was her favorite, the one with the widest satin edge, soft and dreamy between her fingers, and smooth under her cheek.

That day Clee did not go to the garden with her father. She sat on her bed and looked down at the pumpkin patch. Eleven pumpkins wore eleven little blankets. The twelfth pumpkin was bare. It was the biggest pumpkin of all and the last one to be uncovered by the vines.

When dinnertime came Clee wasn't hungry. She sat by her window and watched the wind blowing the dead leaves in circles around the pumpkins. The vines stiffened with cold. Darkness was falling on the garden.

Clee clutched her tiny pumpkin blanket tightly in her hand. Then her fingers loosened. She stroked the satin border one last time.

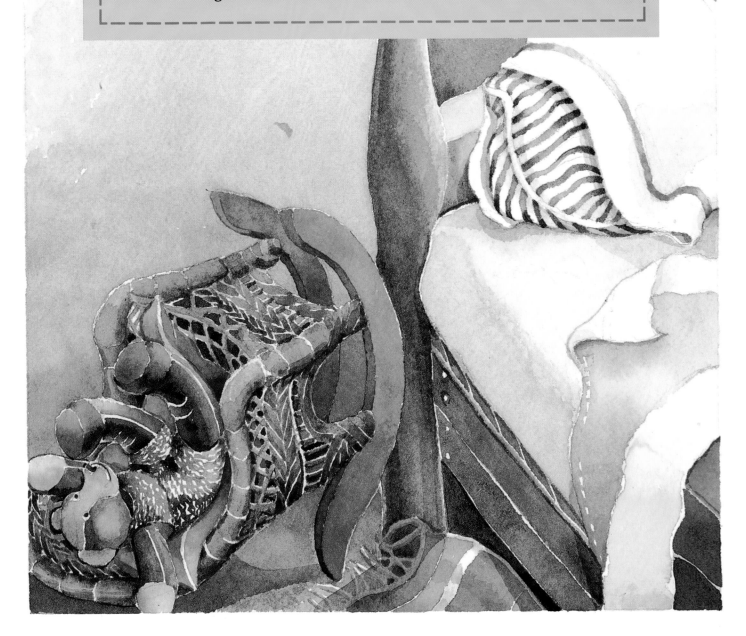

Clee padded down the stairs and out the backdoor. She opened the garden gate and found her way to the pumpkin patch. The wind held its breath. The leaves lay still. Clee tucked her last scrap of pumpkin blanket around the biggest pumpkin of all and ran back to the house before she could change her mind.

Clee missed her pumpkin blanket. She had a new down comforter, but it covered without comforting her. Only the sight of the blank-faced pumpkins in their woolen kerchiefs cheered her. Each of the blanket patches was the same color now—faded by the autumn sun and rain. Each clung to its orange pumpkin like a threadbare hat.

On the evening before Hallowe'en, Clee and her father took the wheelbarrow down to the garden for the last harvest. They separated the brittle vines from the yellow-orange gourds, and Clee imagined sewing her blanket back together. She took the first square from the pumpkin closest. It no longer felt soft and dreamy between her fingers or smooth under her cheek.

Suddenly a gust of wind pulled the scrap right out of Clee's hand carrying it above and beyond her reach. Clee and her father watched the wind flip the pumpkin squares off all the rest of the pumpkins, blowing them high above the birch tree forest. The pumpkin squares tumbled upwards, floating higher and higher on a playful current of wind, into a sparkling sky.

The stars sewed the pieces of Clee's blanket back together with pin-prick threads. When they had finished, the shimmering pumpkin blanket draped itself around a mother-of-pearl pumpkin and the folds winked at Clee from the night sky.

Clee's father lifted her into the wheelbarrow and piled the fat-cheeked pumpkins around her. Clee laughed as they bounced through the garden gate into the house.

That Hallowe'en, twelve lively faces lit Clee's porch. Their eyes and smiles shone far into the night.